6/22/23
19.99

D0989743

Copyright 2021

By Structure & Jesse Byrd Creative Inc.
ALL RIGHTS RESERVED

Seeking Shanti
STORY BY: Jesse Byrd & Sandy Kaur Gill
ILLUSTRATED BY: Mónica Paola Rodríguez
SPECIAL THANKS TO: Ramya Velury, Emma Riley, Sandya Prabhat & Chaaya Prabhat

ISBN: 978-1-223-19149-2 Hardcover
ISBN: 978-1-223-18698-6 Paperback
10 9 8 7 6 5 4 3 2

PUBLISHED BY PAW PRINTS PUBLISHING
PAWPRINTSPUBLISHING.COM
PRINTED IN CHINA

STRUCTURE

Seeking Shanti

A FAMILY'S STORY OF CLIMATE MIGRATION

Written by **Jesse Byrd & Sandy Kaur Gill**

Illustrated by **Mónica Paola Rodríguez**

Special Thanks to **Ramya Velury, Emma Riley, Sandya Prabhat & Chaaya Prabhat**

PAW PRINTS
PUBLISHING

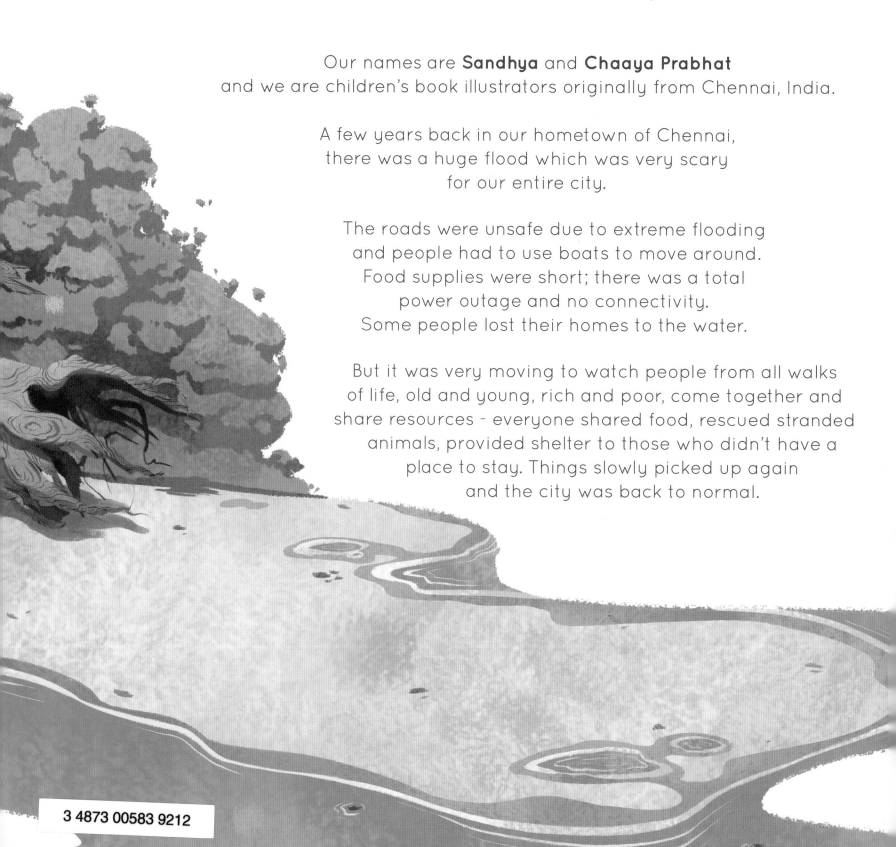

Dear reader and new friend,

Our names are **Sandhya** and **Chaaya Prabhat**
and we are children's book illustrators originally from Chennai, India.

A few years back in our hometown of Chennai,
there was a huge flood which was very scary
for our entire city.

The roads were unsafe due to extreme flooding
and people had to use boats to move around.
Food supplies were short; there was a total
power outage and no connectivity.
Some people lost their homes to the water.

But it was very moving to watch people from all walks
of life, old and young, rich and poor, come together and
share resources - everyone shared food, rescued stranded
animals, provided shelter to those who didn't have a
place to stay. Things slowly picked up again
and the city was back to normal.

From the fires and earthquakes in California to hurricanes and
tropical storms in India, climate disasters affect us all.
We were thrilled to be involved with the creation of **Seeking Shanti**,
sharing our stories and experiences with Jesse and Sandy, each of whom
has also experienced personal loss due to climate crisis and
displacement. Together, we wanted to show how important it is,
when disaster strikes, to work together like **Kavya**, her family,
and her community. In doing so, we can support one another during difficult
times and change the world for the better.

We're making a pact with you and the creative team behind
Seeking Shanti to be *prepared* for a climate disaster.
By preparing, we are doing what we can ahead of time.
And, by sharing information with our friends and family, talking about the
climate crisis, and helping our neighbors when they are in need we are keeping
kindness and community at the center of what we do.

Sincerely,
Sandhya and Chaaya

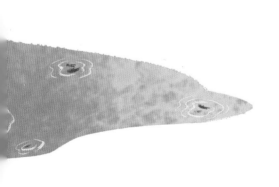

Glossary

Shanti = Peace

Kavya = Poem

Sakhi = Friend

Baba = Dad

Amma = Mom

Dadi = Grandmother

Dada = Grandfather

Chachu = Uncle

Beta = My Child

Kavya bounces up and down as she
races home from school.

"I know I promised to teach you how to play fetch
today, **Sakhi**, and I will," she says.
"I will do it as soon as I get back from
the fish market with **Baba**."

"**Baba**, where are the people?"

"I'm not sure, **beta**. The fish market in **Shanti** never closes this early," **Baba** frowns.

"Maybe the rain scared them away," **Kavya** says.

As **Baba** and **Kavya**
head home,
thunder booms. Clouds burst
with heavier and heavier rain.

Kavya sees **Dadi**
waving nervously from the
shore.

Dadi is dripping wet as she gives them the news.

The rain was even louder now and sounded like hissing snakes.
Kavya could only make out a few of **Dadi**'s words because of the noise.

"A __orm is c_m__g!"

Soon, everyone starts to grab different things.

Dada grabs food.

Baba grabs water.

Dadi grabs clothes.

And **Kavya** packs her most special thing.

"We can't leave **Sakhi**, **Baba**! How will she make it through the storm alone?"
Kavya begs as **Sakhi** pulls on her backpack.

"I'm sorry, **Kavya**, we can't take her.
We need to hurry to meet your uncle before the rain gets worse," **Baba** answers.

Kavya frowns and looks to **Dadi** for help.
Baba looks at them both, sighs, then
waves **Sakhi** into the boat.

As they sail down the rising river, they see a tree.

The tree once stretched high into the sky, but now is sleeping on its side.

"I'm going to help them move the tree," **Baba** yells.

"Me too!" **Kavya** adds.

"How much longer until
we get to **Chachu**'s?" **Kavya** asks.

"I don't know. It may take longer to find
our way with the sun going down,"
Baba replies.

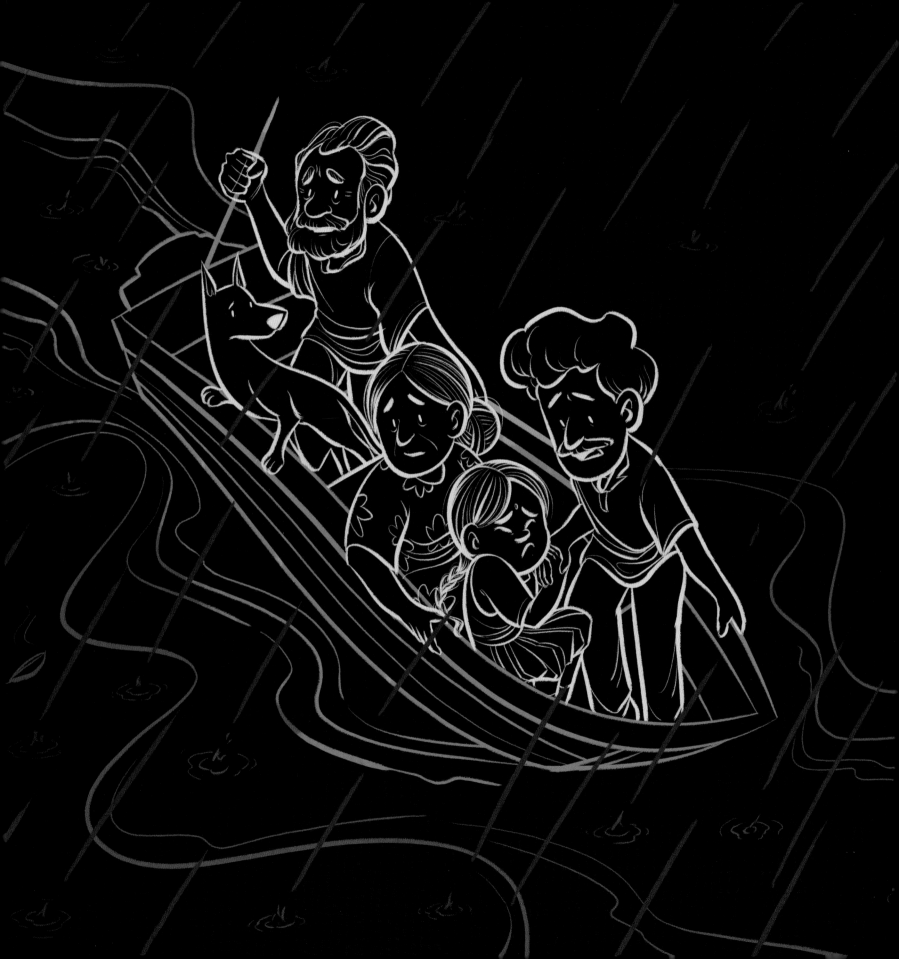

Suddenly,
everything goes dark,
like someone threw a thick blanket over the Earth.

"**Kavya**, sometimes the lights can go out during a storm,"
Baba explains.
"But, don't you worry. Keep your hand in mine and we'll be fine."

Kavya squeezes **Baba**'s hand with both of hers
and shuts her eyes tight.

When **Kavya** opens her eyes, she sees
a beam of light cutting through the night.

"Chachu!"

"Let's push the Jeep out of the mud!" **Chachu** yells.

As they try to move the Jeep,
Baba, **Dadi**, and **Dada** look as if they are being
swallowed into a chocolate milkshake.

"**Baba**, can I help?" **Kavya** shouts.

Just as **Kavya** finishes her sentence, the front wheels grip.
The Jeep jerks forward and is finally set free.

Airplanes roar through the night's sky
like a pack of growling dogs.

Kavya looks out of the window to see her home racing by.

As they drive further into the darkness, **Kavya** feels as if
she is leaving a piece of herself behind.

Chachu takes the family to a place where some people are crying and yelling. Some are sitting with other people and some are sitting alone.

Baba whispers to **Dadi** and **Dada** as **Kavya** lies down, "I don't know if we'll ever get to go home."

Baba teaches
Kavya a trick to
help pass time at
the camp.

Kavya teaches
Sakhi.

"Great news!" **Chachu** finally yells.

"We can go back home to **Shanti**!"

Kavya wiggles with excitement
on their drive back.

But when she arrives home,
it's different than she remembered.

"I don't think we can fix this," **Baba** whispers.
"Should we even try?"

"If **Chachu**'s home is ruined too,
where else will we go?" **Dadi** asks.

Kavya feels her stomach turn as she listens
to their words.

"Our family has been here forever, **Baba**! This is home.
Trips to the fish market.
Dadi taking bananas to the temple every morning.
Sakhi chasing me around the yard.
Family dinners.

Our memories with **Amma**," **Kavya** cries.

Baba still isn't sure if staying is the best thing to do.

But, with a little help,
they choose to stay and try to
rebuild their home.

Because, in the end,
all they want is **Shanti.**

Discussion Questions
For Families/Educators

Introduction Questions

Some questions to discuss with your children or class prior to reading:

1. What is your favorite thing about your home, neighborhood, community, or city?
2. What makes it so special?
3. How would you feel if something happened to it?
4. What is a natural or climate disaster? What do you know about this term?
5. What do you want to know? What makes you curious?

Activity

Primary: Read "Seeking Shanti"
and create your own emergency evacuation checklist and kit.
Think about all of the things you should pack before possibly having to evacuate your home!
Draw or write your items and be sure to color any drawings in!

Here is an example of what Kavya might include in her Emergency List:

Flashligh or another source of light.
Pictures of family, friends, and anything small that comforts her.
Her favorite clothes!
Items that she uses to stay healthy; like a toothbrush.

Any food items that are easy to take with her on the road.

Junior/Intermediate: Read *"Seeking Shanti"*
and write a Persuasive Letter from Kavya to her Baba, convincing him to
either stay in Shanti or start fresh somewhere new.

/ or /

Read *"Seeking Shanti"* and share a moment when
you have been frightened about or by the natural world.

Tell Kavya and her Baba what you did to move through that scary moment,
and how it relates to the experience they've gone through.

Review

- What have you learned about natural disasters and how they affect families around the world?
- What are some things you can do to help prepare for these situations?
- How can you raise awareness for natural disasters and climate change?
- How are these two connected?

Jesse Byrd

Jesse is an **award-winning children's book author, editor, and publisher** who grew up in Oakland, CA and New Orleans, LA. He LOVES being part of creating stories that have a chance to make a difference.

Much like Kavya's experience leaving Shanti, Jesse remembers feeling afraid when his family had to race to escape Hurricane Katrina in New Orleans.

Mónica Paola Rodríguez

Mónica is a **freelance children's book illustrator** who grew up in San Juan, Puerto Rico, where she currently resides. She loves art and helping people bring their stories to life.

Similar to Kavya, Mónica felt very scared when Hurricane Maria hit her home. But by talking to her family and friends, she got the courage to rise up!

Sandy Gill

Sandy is a **Fashion Creative and school teacher** who loves to learn and try new things! She grew up in the beautiful multicultural city of Toronto, Canada and spends her time travelling and helping people feel more confident through fashion.

When she feels afraid, she goes on a long walk with her dog Missy, and like Kavya, she takes her puppy everywhere!

Ramya Velury

Ramya is an **executive producer and artist manager** who grew up in Kentucky and graduated from New York University's Gallatin School of Individualized Study. Now that she lives in Los Angeles, CA, she's passionate about music and amplifying positive platforms.

Any time Ramya is afraid, she listens to her favorite song or playlist until she's not scared anymore.

Emma Riley

Emma is a **leader in climate and brand development.** After a successful early career developing and executing creative strategies, she launched the award-winning organization, Lonely Whale. In January of 2021, she joined Better Shelter and the IKEA Foundation in developing Structure, a climate migrant initiative that creates sustainable, safe and dignified shelter for people who have lost their homes in natural disasters. Visit create-structure.org. Emma is from and resides in the Bay Area.

The rapid rise of wildfires scares her a lot and she finds peace and focus in supporting impactful creative work like *Seeking Shanti*.